A Duck in Luck!

Level 1C

WITHDRAWN

Written by Anne Marie Ryan
with Francis Opuminji

Illustrated by Florencia Denis
Reading Consultant: Betty Franchi

About Phonics

Spoken English uses more than 40 speech sounds. Each sound is called a *phoneme*. Some phonemes relate to a single letter (d-o-g) and others to combinations of letters (sh-ar-p). When a phoneme is written down, it is called a *grapheme*. Teaching these sounds, matching them to their written form, and sounding out words for reading is the basis of phonics.

Early phonics instruction gives children the tools to sound out, blend, and say the words without having to rely on memory or guesswork. This instruction gives children the confidence and ability to read unfamiliar words, helping them progress toward independent reading.

About the Consultant

Betty Franchi is an American educator with
a Bachelor's Degree in Elementary and Middle
Education as well as a Master's Degree in Special
Education. Betty holds a National Boards for
Professional Teaching Standards certification.
Throughout her 24 years as a teacher, she has
studied and developed an expertise in Phonetic
Awareness and has implemented phonetic strategies,
teaching many young children to read, including
students with special needs.

Reading tips

 This book focuses on the sounds:
qu, x, ff, ll, ss, zz, and *ck.*

Tricky and/or new words in this book

Any words in bold may have unusual spellings
or are new and have not yet been introduced.

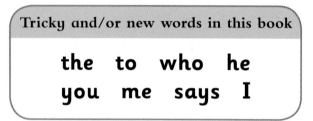

Tricky and/or new words in this book

**the   to   who   he
you   me   says   I**

Extra ways to have fun with this book

After the readers have finished the story, ask them
questions about what they have just read.

What friend does Nick find at the well?
Why does Nick get into a huff?

Make flashcards of the focus sounds (qu, x, ff, ll, ss, zz,
and ck). Ask the reader to say the sounds. This will
help reinforce letter/sound matches.

My big brother
listens to me read.
He says I'm a very good
reader. I like to read in
his bedroom.

A Pronunciation Guide

This grid highlights the sounds used in the story and offers a guide on how to say them.

s as in sat	a as in ant	t as in tin	p as in pig
i as ink	n as in net	c as in cat	e as in egg
h as in hen	r as in rat	m as in mug	d as in dog
g as in get	o as in ox	u as in up	l as in log
f as in fan	b as in bag	j as in jug	v as in van
w as in wet	z as in zip	y as in yet	k as in kit
qu as in quiz	x as in box	ff as in off	ll as in fill
ss as in hiss	zz as in buzz	ck as in duck	

Be careful not to add an /uh/ sound to /s/, /t/, /p/, /c/, /h/, /r/, /m/, /d/, /g/, /l/, /f/ and /b/. For example, say /ff/ not /fuh/ and /sss/ not /suh/.

Nick **the** duck sits on a dock.

Bugs buzz and play in the sky.

Nick wants **to** play as well.

Who will **he** pick?

"Will **you** play with **me**?"
says Nick.

"Not today," says an ox
on the hill.

"I will hide. Find me quick!"
says Nick.

"I will pass," says a hen
on a box.

"You can hide. I will seek you,"
says Nick.

"You will not," says a cat
on a rock.

"Do you skip?" says Nick.

"Not a bit," says a fox as
he zips off.

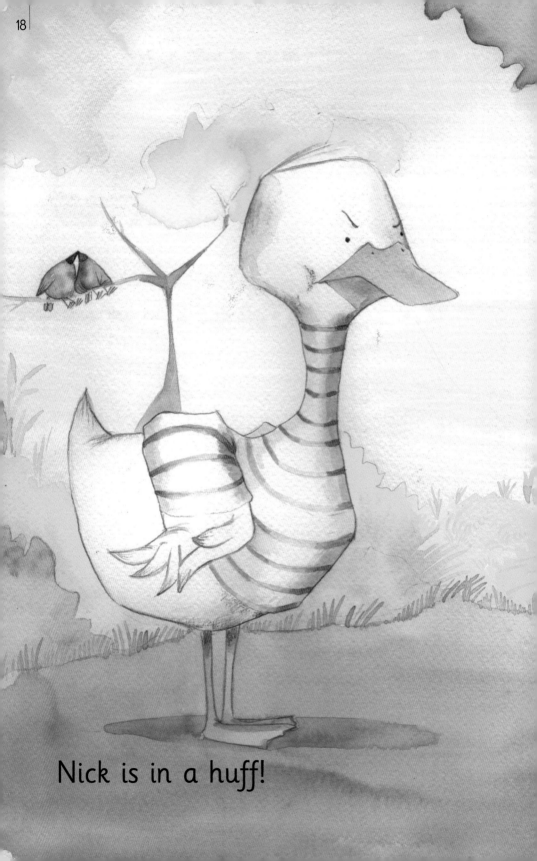

Nick is in a huff!

But Nick is in luck!

Jova is at the well.

"I will play with you,"
says Jova.

"Quack!" says Nick.

48 TITLES IN SIX LEVELS
Betty Franchi recommends...

Other titles to enjoy from Level 1

I love reading phonics — **Bad Rat** — 978 1 84898 747 0

I love reading phonics — **The Best Gift** — 978 1 84898 750 0

I love reading phonics — **Bret and Grandma's Trip!** — 978 1 84898 751 7

Some titles from Level 2

I love reading phonics — **Wish Fish** — 978 1 84898 755 5

I love reading phonics — **Chuck and Duck** — 978 1 84898 756 2

I love reading phonics — **Pink Bunny** — 978 1 84898 760 9

I love reading phonics — **Let's go to the Swings** — 978 1 84898 759 3

Some titles from Level 3

I love reading phonics — **Bart's Go-Cart** — 978 1 84898 768 5

I love reading phonics — **Queen Ella's Feet** — 978 1 84898 764 7

I love reading phonics — **Puff Flies** — 978 1 84898 765 4

I love reading phonics — **The Pop Duet** — 978 1 84898 767 8

An Hachette Company
First Published in the United States by TickTock, an imprint of Octopus Publishing Group.
www.octopusbooksusa.com

Copyright © Octopus Publishing Group Ltd 2013

Distributed in the US by
Hachette Book Group USA
237 Park Avenue, New York NY 10017, USA

Distributed in Canada by
Canadian Manda Group
165 Dufferin Street, Toronto, Ontario, Canada M6K 3H6

ISBN 978 1 84898 749 4

Printed and bound in China
10 9 8 7 6 5 4 3 2 1